Starfish Summer

ONA GRITZ-GILBERT

ILLUSTRATIONS BY YONG CHEN

HARPERCOLLINSPUBLISHERS

Library of Congress Cataloging-in-Publication Data
Gritz-Gilbert, Ona.
    Starfish summer / Ona Gritz-Gilbert ; drawings by Yong Chen.
       p.   cm.
    Summary: A young girl learns how to be more independent from her mother during a summer
at the beach.
    ISBN 0-06-027193-0
    [1. Fear—Fiction.   2. Homesickness—Fiction.   3. Friendship—Fiction.   4. Beaches—
Fiction.   5. Great-aunts—Fiction.]   I. Chen, Yong, ill.   II. Title.
PZ7.G89115St   1998   97-38595
[Fic]—dc21   CIP
                                                                                      AC

1 2 3 4 5 6 7 8 9 10
❖
First Edition

For my father, who gave me a love of the ocean,

and my mother, who gave me a love of words

—O. G. G.

CONTENTS

Treadmill,
Tickle Bottom, Pop Green,
Poke the Jelly

A small boy in a backwards cap stood in front of Amy and stared. He had round, caramel-brown cheeks, and on his nose was a white stripe of zinc. It made her think of a cupcake with icing.

"Crystal!" he called.

A taller girl, pretty with that same caramel skin, came up beside him. Her hair was beaded and braided in a quilted pattern.

The boy pointed his chin in Amy's direction. "Who's that?" he asked.

Crystal rested a hand on one jutted-out hip. "She's the girl staying next door with Miz Martin."

Amy nodded. "My mom's aunt Jenny."

Crystal gave Amy a slow up-down look. "You know how to play treadmill?"

Amy shook her head and studied her flip-flops.

"How 'bout tickle bottom or pop green?"

"Poke the jelly?" the little boy added.

"Unh-unh," Amy said to the Band-Aid on her left knee.

"How you gonna live at the ocean if you don't know anything about it?" asked Crystal.

"What *do* you know?" the boy put in.

Amy chewed a piece of hair and thought a moment. "I know hopscotch; ring-a-levio; freeze tag; Mother, may I?; red light green light; steal the bacon; and dodgeball."

"Sidewalk games," said Crystal. "We're talking about beach stuff."

"My sister and me do ring-a-levio and all that when summer's over," the little boy explained.

Crystal nodded. "In the schoolyard."

"I won't be here after the summer," Amy told them. "I'll be back with my mom in New York."

Crystal shook her head and looked at her brother. "C'mon, Raymond; she doesn't know anything about anything."

Amy watched while Crystal and Raymond walked to the edge of the water, where the tide pulled the sand backwards beneath them.

"Treadmill," Raymond called to Amy.

Crystal stood on one foot and held out the other so the water barely grazed it like feathering fingers. Next, she grasped Raymond's hand to balance him while he did the same.

"Tickle bottom," Raymond explained, turning to Amy.

Amy followed slowly as they walked along the shoreline hunting for something in the sand.

"Here, Raymond," Crystal said, handing him a tangle of seaweed. He broke off a piece and gave it to Amy. It was covered with blistery pods, and when she pressed them they burst like the bumps in bubble wrap.

"Pop green," Amy named the game.

Crystal glanced at her coolly over her shoulder, then poked at a washed-up jellyfish with a driftwood stick.

"Poke the jelly," Amy mumbled with a shrug. She reached down to gather beach glass, but when Crystal and Raymond headed for the boardwalk, she found herself following them.

On the splintery boardwalk, old people sat

3

facing the beach as if it were a play they were watching.

"So tall!" one cried when she saw Crystal.

"And Raymond!" added another. "When'd you get to be all elbows and knees?"

"We just seen them all, day before yesterday," Raymond whispered to Amy. "They're always acting like we've grown since last time."

She wanted to ask him why his sister didn't like her, but a bunch of questions from the old people got in the way.

"Enjoying yourself, sweetie?"

"Great-Aunt Jenny taking care of you okay?"

"What's a big-city girl think of our little seaside town?"

"So brave, away from your mother all summer."

Amy mumbled answers to her Band-Aid, dangling now like a pull tab. "I'm old enough. I wanted to come."

"Such a shy one!" a lady in a floppy hat exclaimed.

A woman with gray woolly hair and windpink cheeks looked at Amy and sighed. "The image of her mother at that age."

"That's Mrs. Goldman," Raymond told Amy.

"And Mattie Stone in the floppy hat."

"You've seen the dolls your great-aunt Jenny makes out of undergarments?" Mattie Stone asked.

"Socks, Mattie." Aunt Jenny came over with her sewing bag slung on her shoulder. Her braids, dyed from a package she called "canned youth," shone the color of rust in the sun. She sat down next to a thin woman in men's overalls. "I make dolls out of socks!"

The overalls woman gave Amy a wink. "Beautiful dolls, I might add." Her skin looked like a sheet of paper that had been crumpled in a ball and smoothed out again.

Aunt Jenny pulled a skein of new wool from her bag. "Just keeping myself busy," she said.

"Mrs. Fine's right." Crystal squeezed onto the bench between the two women and held up her hands in cat's cradle position. "Miz Martin, you make great sock dolls."

Aunt Jenny placed the yarn over Crystal's fingers. "My biggest fan." She grinned.

"Miz Martin can spin a ball in twelve and three quarter minutes," Raymond said to Amy. "Crystal timed her."

In the middle of the chatter, one man sat

smiling, gazing over their heads and beyond. Amy thought he had beautiful eyes—soft, sky-colored marbles. At his feet, a dark-haired dog lay asleep, curled like a braided throw rug.

"That's Mr. Fine," Raymond whispered loudly. "He's blind."

A chill crawled up Amy's spine like a spider.

"It's getting cool outside," the blind man mentioned, as though he'd seen her shiver.

"Cool enough to ride?" Raymond asked his sister.

Crystal nodded. "Miz Martin, do you need me for any more winding?"

"I'm fine," Aunt Jenny told her. "You go on."

Amy listened to the whir of bicycle wheels against the slats of the boardwalk as Crystal and Raymond rode off. Crystal had already said Amy didn't know anything about anything. What would she say when she found out Amy couldn't even ride a bike?

TWO

Mama's Girl

The attic room where Amy slept in Aunt Jenny's house was peopled with sock dolls. One wore a violet pantsuit and had bright brown beads for eyes and a small red bead for a navel. Another, in a long black peasant dress, hung on the wall like a picture. There was also a pair of twins with argyle faces sitting on the windowsill in matching Christmas-red sweat suits. Aunt Jenny told Amy a few of their names each night, but at the moment she couldn't remember any. Outside the window, the waves kept crashing. It felt as if at any moment they'd cover the house and wash it away.

The phone on the bedside table rang, as it did every night exactly at eight thirty. And as she did

every night, Amy waited a few rings before answering. It hurt to have Mom's voice so close in her ear and not feel Mom's arm warm on her shoulder. She found she missed the funniest things. Not just the feel of Mom's hugs but their smell, like a loaf of oatmeal bread baking. *Mama's girl*—that's what the kids at school called Amy.

Mama's girl. And it was true. She didn't know how *not* to tell Mom everything. Even when the kids started calling her that, the first thing she did was come home and cry about it to Mom.

"They're envious," Mom assured her. "Not every family is as close as you and I."

Then, when the kids teased her because she couldn't ride a bike, she not only told Mom what they said, she admitted how scared the idea of riding made her. Mom responded that if she was afraid to do something, she shouldn't feel she had to.

"Riding a bike really is dangerous," Mom said,

"especially in New York. The sidewalks are too crowded, and I wouldn't even think of letting you ride in the street. You're absolutely right not to want to ride, Amy."

Usually, Mom's words of comfort made Amy feel better. This time, though, she had hoped that for once Mom would help her be brave. Amy was tired of being a frightened mama's girl. She wanted to be able to stand up to people instead of always running home to Mom. She wanted to be able to get on a bike like everyone else and learn to ride.

So when Mom told Amy about the special training she needed for work, Amy said she should go. Even though it meant Mom would be three thousand miles away for the whole summer and Amy would have to stay with her great-aunt Jenny, whom she hardly knew.

"When I was little, I spent all my summers with Aunt Jenny," Mom had told her. "I know you'll love being by the ocean." But she studied Amy with eyes that shone like underwater stones. "Oh, sweetie, I wouldn't even consider going away for so long if it didn't mean a promotion when I got home."

"I'll be fine with Aunt Jenny, really," Amy

insisted. "I want you to go."

Since Amy's dad had died when she was a baby, it was up to Mom to work and pay for everything. Amy understood that a promotion would help. But that wasn't the reason she told Mom to go. *Mama's girl.* This was a chance for her to start over, be on her own, and make new friends. No one could say she was a mama's girl after she'd been away from her "mama" all summer.

As soon as Amy arrived, Aunt Jenny told her there was a girl her age living right next door. *Great,* thought Amy. Maybe she'd make a friend who'd think she was brave for being so far from home. But only the old people saw Amy that way. Crystal just didn't seem to want her there. Worse, Amy was still a mama's girl. Having Mom three thousand miles away made her feel like a piece of herself was missing. Only one thing had changed. Every night, when Amy picked up the phone, she lied to her mother.

Amy couldn't admit how homesick she was. Instead, she described tickle bottom, pop green, and poke the jelly, and pretended Crystal was her best friend.

"Sometimes we let her baby brother, Raymond, play," she told Mom tonight. "But it's better when it's just us, really."

"It's silly of me to worry so much," Mom said. "You're doing great, honey."

"Thanks," Amy mumbled, twisting the curling phone cord around her finger. "I miss you, though."

"It's sweet of you to say that," Mom answered, "but I remember what it's like to be young and busy with your friends. You probably wouldn't even think about me if I didn't pester you every night with phone calls."

"No, really, Mom. I do." It was so hard not to blurt out the words *Please come get me*. Amy knew Mom would forget her promotion and fly there tomorrow if she asked. But Amy couldn't do that to Mom. "Listen, I better go. I love you."

The waves seemed to get louder as Amy climbed into bed. She switched off her lamp, and a porch light flickering from across the street turned Aunt Jenny's dolls into a crowd of angry strangers. Which was worse, Amy wondered, a mama's girl or a liar?

"You asleep yet?" Aunt Jenny asked from the doorway.

"Unh-unh," Amy answered.

"It always took me a good few days before I

could really sleep in a strange place." Aunt Jenny
sat on the edge of Amy's bed. "Until I developed
my special trick, that is."

With her rust-colored braids coming loose
and her face shadowed in the low gleam of the
across-the-street porch light, Aunt Jenny looked
like the girl in *Anne of Green Gables*.

"You mean like counting sheep?" Amy asked.
"Or naming sock dolls?"

"No, counting always keeps me awake," Aunt Jenny said. "The trick is to turn the unfamiliar into the familiar. Want to try it?"

"Okay." Up close, Aunt Jenny smelled like tangerines and yellowed books. *Not the same as baking oatmeal bread,* Amy thought, *but still cozy.*

"Good. Now, what's outside your window at home?"

"Just the street," Amy answered.

"But on your corner is Broadway. So on warm nights when the window's open, what do you hear? Traffic?"

Amy nodded. "And car alarms and sirens."

"So that's what you're used to," Aunt Jenny said. "Now listen to the ocean, but imagine that the waves are really cars whooshing by on Broadway." She stood up and tucked the summer quilt around Amy's shoulders. "And if the birds start singing and wake you up too early, just pretend they're horns beeping."

Amy worked on turning the waves into a rush of cars on a wet city street. The porch light became the street lamp below her New York window. The next thing she knew, it was morning.

THREE

Endless-as-the-Ocean Eyes

Every day, Amy watched as Crystal and Raymond played treadmill, tickle bottom, pop green, and poke the jelly. Sometimes she brought a dusty book from Aunt Jenny's shelves. Sometimes she busied herself carving sand statues. *Today*, she'd tell herself each morning. *Today Crystal will call me over to play.*

If Crystal and her brother waded in the water, Amy went in too, staying off to the side. By listening to the lessons Crystal gave Raymond, she learned to let the ocean roll on her hip instead of smacking her belly, and to rise to meet a wave instead of ducking down.

It seemed to Amy that Crystal could do anything. Barefoot on the beach, Crystal looked as if she were strolling on a thick carpet, but whenever Amy stepped out of her flip-flops, bits of broken shell dug into her heels. If Crystal shook out her towel, her movements were as graceful as a dancer's. When Amy tried it, she set loose a cloud of sand that settled on Crystal like a stinging hailstorm. When Crystal splashed a peach pit in the water with a ballplayer's pitch, Amy tossed a chocolate wrapper. It landed next to Crystal, who gave her a lecture on littering.

"I saw you do it with your peach pit," Amy defended herself.

"Even my baby brother knows fruit pits turn right into sand. Wrappers mess up the beach forever."

Raymond nodded sadly at Amy.

"I didn't know." Amy picked up her wrapper and walked off to gather other pieces of trash she saw lying around.

Crystal started digging in the pudding-soft sand close to the water, while Raymond scouted the shoreline for treasures. When he returned, he pulled Amy over to admire his finds. Her favorites were black, tear-shaped shells with pearly blue watercolor paintings on the inside.

Without glancing at Amy, Crystal asked Raymond if he'd care for dessert. In a voice that made Amy think of lacy, old-fashioned dresses, she described the rich filling in her chocolate sand surprise.

"Your brother brings you the loveliest jewels," Amy told Crystal, trying to add some lace trim to her voice.

"I thought I heard someone say something," Crystal continued speaking to Raymond. "Must just be the waves."

Raymond gave Amy a shrug and held out his spoon with the make-believe treat. "Wanna taste?"

She shook her head and trudged toward the boardwalk, where the audience always seemed to be watching a scene quite different from the one she was living.

"Look at that threesome!" Amy heard Aunt Jenny say again and again.

"Such energy," Mrs. Fine would tell Mrs. Goldman.

"Just watching those three makes me tired," Mattie Stone would add.

When Amy got to the top of the splintery steps, she saw Mr. Fine standing at the railing. Rascal, his guide dog, seemed to be staring right through her. She wished she'd stayed where she was.

"Tell me, Amy," Mr. Fine called. "What color is the water today?"

Amy felt the chill spiders crawling. *How does he know it's me?*

She peered past him at Crystal charging the waves. "It's just gray."

"Hmmmm." Mr. Fine leaned comfortably against a rail post and Rascal leaned comfortably against his legs. Amy hoped that didn't mean they were settling in for a long talk.

"You've been with us now . . . a week?" Mr. Fine asked. Rascal yawned and lay down.

"Uh-huh." Amy sighed. A whole week, and Crystal was still as sharp and cold as the salt water when you first step in.

Mr. Fine gazed in the direction of the ocean. "It's not always easy making friends."

Amy stared in startled silence. She knew deaf people could read lips. But could the blind read minds?

"Everyone else thinks Crystal and me are

17

already friends," she admitted to her flip-flops.

"People tend to see only what they want to," Mr. Fine told her. "Especially us old folk."

Mr. Fine is a kind man, Amy thought. She just wished it didn't make her so nervous to see his endless-as-the-ocean eyes. She turned and looked at the real ocean again, not just where Crystal played in the waves, but beyond to where the sun played too.

"The water's mostly greeny-gray with silver jewelry," she said. "And it's wearing a silver belt over where Europe begins."

She glanced at Mr. Fine, who aimed a smile slightly over her head. Though she still couldn't help turning quickly away, for the first time that week, she smiled too.

FOUR

The Magical Thing
About Starfish

A my glanced out her bedroom window and saw Raymond and his parents in their driveway. His dad was fitting a cooler into their open hatchback, while his mama tugged a comb through Raymond's hair. Amy had never seen him without his backwards cap before. Instead of his usual sandy swimming trunks, Raymond had on a pressed shirt tucked neatly into fresh jeans. He looked up and called "Hey" to Amy, just as Crystal slammed out of the house in a lime-colored sundress.

"Hi, Raymond," Amy answered shyly.

"We gotta go to our grandma's," he told her.

"You don't need to announce it to the whole block," Crystal snapped at Raymond. "'Specially to neighbors who don't keep their noses in their own houses."

"I was just saying hello," Amy mumbled, closing the window.

With the beach to herself, Amy gathered seaweed to play pop green. It looked like canned spinach, so she threw it down. She tried making chocolate sand surprise, but that didn't work either. Instead of pudding, the sand close to the water felt like nothing but mud. The ocean seemed too large, like it might swallow her up, and she knew if she went in, the salty taste would remind her of tears. She spent the rest of the morning alone on the stairs of the splintery boardwalk, while the old people chatted and dozed.

Finally, Mr. Fine came to the railing, lifting his chin toward the sun. "The breeze feels beautiful," he said.

Amy picked at a boardwalk splinter on her finger. "It's nice."

"What would you say to a walk on the beach?" he asked.

"Okay." She shrugged.

Mr. Fine offered his hand to help Amy stand.

Could blindness be catching? She shivered at the thought of his touch.

"I'm all right," she said, jumping up quickly.

"What a nice idea, Arthur." Mrs. Fine rushed over with Rascal, who guided Mr. Fine as he felt his way down each step. "It's a perfect day for a stroll."

Amy flushed. She'd seen Mrs. Fine touch her husband's shoulder and tuck her hand in his elbow when they went for a walk. And nothing bad had happened to her. Mrs. Fine's eyes still saw the ocean.

"Just one more step," Amy said, as Rascal brought Mr. Fine to the end of the stairs.

"Have a good time," called Mrs. Fine, rejoining her friends.

Amy left her flip-flops next to Mr. Fine's sandals. They made their way past the hot sand and walked along the cool shoreline.

"Treadmill!" Amy shouted, feeling a tug backwards beneath her. Forgetting to be afraid of his touch, she pulled Mr. Fine over so he could stand in the exact right spot.

"My, it *is* a treadmill. What do you think of that, buddy?" Mr. Fine asked Rascal. The dog waved his tail in response.

Next, Amy helped Mr. Fine stand on one foot

and hold up the other so the water could play tickle bottom on his heel.

"Oh, that tickles," he laughed.

With a small pleading sound, Rascal gave him a nudge.

"Go on." Mr. Fine removed the dog's special harness. "I'll be all right here with my friend."

Rascal entered the water. Soon only his head could be seen, bobbing like a buoy on the swells.

"So, how do you know these wonderful beach games?" Mr. Fine asked Amy.

She burrowed her toes in the sand. "They're Crystal and Raymond's. I just copied them."

As they walked along, Amy concentrated on making heavy-man footprints while Mr. Fine listened to gull calls and took deep sea-air breaths.

"Look!" she called, coming upon a starfish. Then she covered her mouth. How could she say that, knowing he was blind!

"Let's see," Mr. Fine said, making her feel instantly better. He held out an open palm.

Amy closed her eyes as she passed him the starfish so she could see it through his eyes. It felt like breaded chicken in her hand.

"Ah," said Mr. Fine. "We used to call these fallen stars." He gave the starfish back to her. "Do you know the magical thing about them?"

Amy shook her head, then remembered he wouldn't be able to see her. "Unh-unh," she said.

"If that starfish were still alive and it lost an arm, another would grow in its place. Isn't that marvelous?"

"I wish that could happen to people," Amy said, glancing at Mr. Fine's eyes.

"Oh, but it does, Amy, it does. Think how people come in and out of your life."

Amy thought of her mom, how she missed her like an arm from her own body. "You can't grow another person," she said.

"No, that's right, you can't. That would be like trying to replace part of your heart. But believe me, Amy, those empty spaces get filled in unexpected ways."

Amy had hoped Crystal would be there to fill her empty spaces, but it definitely wasn't turning out that way. "How can a person hate you before even knowing you?" she blurted, plopping down onto the sand.

"They can't, so their feelings must not really be about you." Mr. Fine crouched beside her. "And something tells me it's not hate Crystal's feeling."

"Then why does she treat me so bad?"

"I think she's just protecting herself."

"From me?" Amy stared at him wide-eyed. "I'm not scary."

Mr. Fine rubbed his chin and nodded. Amy could feel him searching for the right words. "Newness is scary. And so is the idea of getting close to someone, especially if you know they'll eventually be leaving."

Amy raked ragged lines in the sand with her fingers. "Well, I wish she'd just be nicer to me."

"It's hard for her," Mr. Fine said. "Crystal gets very attached to people."

Amy frowned. "I don't mind if she gets attached to me."

"But she does. She knows the summer won't be here forever, and neither will you."

"That's not my fault," Amy grumbled.

Mr. Fine sighed. "True."

For a long moment, they were silent. Rascal bounded over and shook himself, creating the quickest of sun showers. Mr. Fine put his harness back on.

"You know, Amy," Mr. Fine said, as they were heading back to the boardwalk. "When a new arm grows on a starfish and fills the empty space, it doesn't happen right away. Like anything worth having, it takes time."

Ooh, Yum!

The next morning when Amy woke, she couldn't help poking her head out the window. Crystal and Raymond were on their stoop, chatting and laughing.

Fine, Amy thought. *I don't need them.* She took the sock doll in the peasant dress down from the wall and brought her over to the bedside table. The layer of dust on the table surface worked perfectly as sand. Amy added her starfish and a fistful of tiny shells and stones. Then she turned on the lamp, releasing a shining circle that looked like glimmering water.

"The ocean feels wonderful today," she made the doll say in her best lacy voice. "Where is everybody?"

Soon the doll was surrounded by her sock doll

friends, faces toward the lightbulb sun, enjoying the glorious beach day.

"Shall we let the Argyle Twins join us?" Janet in the violet pantsuit asked.

"Oh, I suppose," Maria, dressed like a Spanish dancer, answered.

Amy sighed, bored with the game and angry at herself. She hadn't agreed to spend the summer here so she could hide up in her room, playing with dolls like a baby. The idea was to be brave enough to make new friends.

Amy dressed and forced herself to walk next door. Crystal was reading a book, while Raymond studied a spoon.

"How come when you look at yourself in this you're upside down?" Raymond asked.

"I've been meaning to tell you your face is on wrong," Crystal told him.

"Hey, Crystal. Hey, Raymond," Amy mumbled toward the stoop.

Raymond looked up from his upside-down reflection. "Hi, Amy."

Crystal kept her eyes on her book. "You eat breakfast yet?" she asked.

"Unh-unh," Amy answered.

"What are you gonna have?"

Amy stepped closer, surprised that Crystal was speaking to her. "Probably cornflakes and bananas."

"We're going visiting," Crystal said.

"Ooh, yum." Raymond patted his belly and grinned.

Amy didn't know what Crystal meant by "visiting," but she couldn't help wanting to come. "Sounds fun," she told her flip-flops.

Raymond grinned at Amy. "It is. Wanna come?"

Crystal glared at him.

"Three bellies can eat more than two," he said.

Crystal let out a long sigh. "You can come *this* time," she agreed reluctantly.

Raymond and Crystal waited on the walk while Amy ran inside to tell Aunt Jenny.

"I'm skipping breakfast today," she said.

"Oh, you're going visiting. That's nice, Amy."

Aunt Jenny frowned over the last stitches on a steel-gray sock doll. It was layered in Gypsy skirts and had wild gold hair made from the braided rope of drape ties. Amy had picked out the pieces from the giant scrap basket Aunt Jenny kept under the stairs.

Aunt Jenny bit her thread and studied the finished doll.

"This one insists her name is Sybil."

She walked across the room and placed it on the breakfront. Then she arranged the doll's legs and stood back, shaking her head. "I hate the name Sybil."

"You didn't eat anything, did you?" Raymond asked when Amy came back out.

"Unh-unh," she answered.

"Good." Crystal walked ahead. "We'll start at Mrs. Goldman's."

Just Visiting

Mrs. Goldman lived three doors down in a large gray house that needed painting. The front door was open, so Crystal called through the screen.

"Hey, Mrs. Goldman, it's us. Can we come in?"

Mrs. Goldman scurried around as if they were important guests. "I'm so glad you came to visit. Come, come. You must be starving, my *bubbies*."

They filed past the heavy living-room furniture into the bright yellow kitchen.

"Let's see. . . ." Mrs. Goldman fretted into the fridge. "I have cheese blintzes, but they're frozen. There's plenty of applesauce, though, and sour cream. And latkes! I made these fresh just yesterday, I promise."

Raymond turned to Amy. "Lat-keys are potato

pancakes," he explained.

The blintzes went into the oven and the latkes over the stove, while somehow the rest of the refrigerator's contents made it to the table.

"Let's sprinkle a little sugar on the melon, shall we? It will be our little secret." Mrs. Goldman served the children.

Amy took a fork and broke into her blintzes. Rich cheese leaked from the warm dough.

"You have to have sour cream on that, *bubeleh*," Mrs. Goldman insisted. Using a huge soup spoon, she gave Amy a cloudlike glob. "You'll think you're in heaven."

The cool tangy cream and the hot sweet cheese blended together better than anything Amy had ever tasted.

"This is wonderful, Mrs. Goldman," Amy said.

Raymond swung his legs and hummed while he finished off the latkes. "Sure is," he agreed.

Mrs. Goldman's pink cheeks grew pinker with pleasure. "If I'd known you were coming, I'd have made sure to have food in the house. I'm just glad I was able to throw together a little something."

Next, they crossed the street to the Fines' house.

"How is everyone?" Mr. Fine asked the air over their heads.

"We're good," Raymond answered.

"Just visiting," Crystal explained.

"This guy better come with me." Mr. Fine ushered Rascal ahead of him into the den. "He's plump enough without joining in on a visiting session."

"I'm sure you must be hungry." Mrs. Fine fussed over the company. "And I have real bagels, fresh from the bakery."

She set party plates on the front porch table, piling them with pumpernickel, poppy seed, and cinnamon raisin bagels. Then she brought out a mound of cream cheese with broken bits of walnuts inside and a huge bowl of fruit salad.

"Ooh," Amy cried. "I love strawberries."

Mrs. Fine cut up a berry and laid the pieces on a half bagel smothered in cheese. They looked like rose petals resting in snow.

"Iss ez sue ood," said Raymond.

"Don't talk with your mouth full," Crystal scolded.

"This is so good," Raymond repeated after swallowing.

The familiar feeling of homesickness, forgotten since this morning, crashed over Amy like a sudden wave breaking. "My mom and me always have bagels on Sundays," she found herself saying.

"Oh, that's an old-time tradition," Mrs. Fine told her. "Mr. Fine loves nothing better than bagels and the Sunday *Times*."

"But how can he read the paper and eat?" asked Raymond.

Crystal kicked him under the table to head off his words, but they made it to the finish line anyway. "Doesn't he need his hands to read? Ow! Crystal! Stop it."

"I read it to him." Mrs. Fine passed around glasses of ice tea. "It's nicer that way."

Amy thought of the Sunday paper spread on her floor at home. She could hear Mom saying, "Listen to this!" and calling out crazy headlines. She wondered if a starfish could be as lonely for its missing arm as she was for her mom right now. After all, a starfish still had four other arms.

"My mom and me read the paper together too," she said.

Suddenly, Mrs. Fine jumped up from the table. "I just remembered I have cheesecake in the freezer. It won't take but a moment to thaw."

"I'll never, ever, EVER eat again." Raymond held his belly as they started up the street.

"I feel like my stomach's walking ahead of me," said Crystal.

Amy felt full but happy. She finally belonged with the two of them. "Maybe we should go in the water and work it off," she suggested.

Crystal stopped to stare at her. "Are you kidding? We'd sink."

"Probably drown," added Raymond.

Crystal shook her head at Amy. "You really don't know anything about anything."

Amy felt her cheeks heat up. Everything was going so well. Why did she have to say the wrong thing?

They started past the lavenders and pinks of Mattie Stone's prize garden. Amy noticed a floppy hat floating among the flowers.

"Hi, Miz Stone," she called quickly, as a way to change the subject.

"No!" Crystal and Raymond whisper-shouted at the same time.

Mattie Stone glanced up from her weeding and studied the children.

"You've been visiting, haven't you?" she accused them. "Well, don't think you're going to pass over my house. You're going to have honey muffins and my famous Mississippi mud pie. Now!"

Crystal and Raymond groaned and trudged up the walk. As Amy trailed behind, she imagined telling Mattie Stone, "We're just too full to eat any more. We'll have to come back tomorrow." Crystal and Raymond would be grateful, and they'd squeeze Amy clam-tight between them as they walked home.

In real life, though, Amy was afraid to speak up to Mattie Stone. Amy—the mama's girl—always afraid of something.

No One Asked You

The next morning, Amy sat with Aunt Jenny on the porch swing, a rusted metal loveseat on rickety chains. She held a book in her lap, but her mind was somewhere else. It was in Aunt Jenny's garage, behind boxes of gardening tools and breakable china dishes. There, leaning against the wall like a dare, was a bicycle.

"Aunt Jenny, have you ever been afraid of anything?"

"Dogs," Aunt Jenny answered, glancing up from her sewing. "I always think they're out looking for trouble. Except Rascal, of course," she added, biting her thread. "He's gainfully employed."

Amy kicked her feet, and the swing squeaked forward. "I mean have you ever been afraid to *do* something?"

Aunt Jenny studied the face of the unfinished doll in her lap as though it might help her remember. "Horseback riding," she announced with a nod. "I once went on vacation to a dude ranch, and I was afraid to go horseback riding."

"Did you finally do it?" Amy asked.

Aunt Jenny shook her head and continued her sewing. "I waited on the beginner's line and went so far as to get on a horse. He just seemed so tall. I was absolutely sure all he wanted to do was throw me off him."

Amy pictured the bicycle again. It was pretty tall too. "Were you glad in the end that you decided not to ride?" she asked. "Did you have a good time anyway?"

"To this day I regret it," Aunt Jenny said. "After all, what's this life for if not to tip your hat at your fears and then go experience what you can despite them?"

Amy scuffed her flip-flops against the floorboards. Aunt Jenny's answer was so different from what Mom would have said, but it made sense. She'd be really disappointed in herself if she didn't at least try to ride that bicycle.

Still, how could Amy teach herself with everyone out on their stoops watching? It wasn't so much the old people she minded; it was Crystal and Raymond. Crystal was sure to have something mean to say, and even if Raymond was nice about it, he was just a little kid. A little kid who could ride already!

And there they were in front of Aunt Jenny's, as if they had heard Amy thinking about them.

"Hi, Miz Martin," Crystal called.

"Hi, Amy," added Raymond.

"Hey, kids," Aunt Jenny said. "What are you up to?"

"We're going to Mr. Fine's to hear the story," answered Crystal.

"Arthur's talking book from the Library for the Blind," Aunt Jenny explained to Amy. "Can you hear it?"

Amy tilted her head. A murmur like a radio voice hummed through the bushes.

"You should come," Raymond told her. "It's like somebody reading to you, only better."

"No thanks." This was a chance Amy just couldn't pass up. If Crystal and Raymond were inside at the Fines' listening to a whole book, they wouldn't be watching her first attempt at bicycle riding. "I have something to do."

Crystal and Raymond shrugged and walked on.

Amy went inside to change out of her flip-flops. Minutes later, she poked her head out the window.

"Aunt Jenny, have you seen any of my socks?"

"White anklets?" Aunt Jenny asked. "With sailboats on the cuffs? Look down."

The flower box, which had always sat empty, was planted with six tiny sock dolls in sailboat T-shirts.

"I couldn't help it." Aunt Jenny grinned.

Laughing, Amy pulled her sneakers on sockless and came back outside. She took a deep breath and marched toward the garage.

Amy straddled the bike and stood in the street. When she lifted herself onto the seat, only one leg still reached the ground, and that foot was on tiptoe. Nervously, she propped her other foot up on the pedal.

"Now go," she commanded, but her body seemed to be stuck in a game of freeze tag.

"Just get used to it," she coaxed herself. She slid off the seat and walked a few feet with the bike like a hobbyhorse underneath her. Finally, she placed her foot on the higher pedal and pushed down. The bicycle moved forward, but

before she could get her other foot in position,
she landed with a thud on the ground.

"You okay?" Crystal peered down at Amy from
the Fines' top step.

"Yeah." Embarrassed, Amy got up.

"That bike's too big for you," Crystal observed.

Amy glared at her. "I thought you were sup-
posed to be busy with *story hour*," she said, trying
to make it sound like something she was too
grown-up and important to do.

"We are," Raymond answered. "We're listening through the window."

"Figures," Amy mumbled. They wouldn't go

inside and sit on a couch like normal kids. Crystal might miss an opportunity to make her feel miserable.

"You should really wear a helmet," Crystal continued.

Amy decided she'd had enough bike riding for today. It was hard enough trying to teach herself without Crystal making comments. She picked the bike up and began walking it back to Aunt Jenny's.

"Hey, Amy," Crystal called. "We could teach you to ride if you want."

Amy paused but didn't turn around. Why was Crystal being so nice all of a sudden? *It has to be a trick,* she decided. *A way to get me to look even more like a fool.*

"No one asked you," she answered, starting home again.

"Suit yourself," Crystal muttered after her.

EIGHT

Doll Block

"Crystal and I have gone visiting every morning," Amy told her mom. "I would have gained a hundred pounds if it wasn't for all the swimming we're doing."

Amy stayed so busy thinking up new lies, she didn't notice at first when a change came over Aunt Jenny. Yet it was as if the ocean laid down like a quiet gray blanket, or traces of sand stopped finding their way into people's clothes. Aunt Jenny had stopped making sock dolls.

In all the time Amy was there, Aunt Jenny never bothered with dumb chores like cleaning. Now she pinned back her braids and muttered to Amy about dust motes.

"I like the dust," Amy told her, thinking of

her beach game with the sock dolls. "It makes everything soft."

But Aunt Jenny marched through the rooms with a pail sloshing over with water and peppermint soap.

Next, Aunt Jenny made blueberry pancakes.

"I didn't know you could cook," Amy commented, as the pancakes warmed the house with their gold sweet smell. But when she sat down to eat one, her fork broke into sticky raw dough.

"At least you're good at cornflakes," she said.

Mostly, Aunt Jenny just paced. Amy sat and watched until she felt dizzy. She was so worried, she wondered if she should tell Mom when she called. Then she had a better idea.

Amy could ask Crystal for help! Crystal liked Aunt Jenny, and since she lived next door, she'd know if anything like this had happened before. Once they were working together to cure Aunt Jenny, maybe Crystal would forget the way Amy had acted over the bicycle. Maybe they could still become friends.

Amy found Crystal and Raymond munching popcorn on the Fines' stoop.

"Can I sit here?" she asked a swollen mosquito bite on Crystal's shin.

Raymond inched over to give Amy room. Crystal bounced popcorn in the palm of her hand.

Amy sat stiffly. Rascal ambled over, sniffed the popcorn bowl, and settled heavily. Crystal scratched his ears, and Rascal sighed. Then he started snoring.

Amy took a deep breath. "I need to tell you guys something."

Raymond scooted closer to listen better. Crystal stared at the snowball bush that sat on the Fines' grass like a fat bouquet.

"Aunt Jenny dusted her house today," Amy told them.

"I never seen her clean." Raymond's eyes widened.

"With soap," Amy continued. "Then she tried making blueberry pancakes."

Crystal didn't say anything, but her eyebrows met in a worried look.

"And I never EVER saw her use a stove," Raymond added solemnly.

"I didn't tell you the worst part." Amy leaned forward, and this time both Crystal and Raymond tightened around her. "It's been three days since Aunt Jenny worked on a sock doll."

For a moment, the only sound was the breathing rhythm of the ocean.

"Doll block," Mr. Fine's voice announced from the front-porch window.

"What's a doll block?" Raymond asked.

Amy pictured a street just like their beach block, only instead of people, sock dolls chatted on the boardwalk, made blintzes, and played talking book stories from their windows.

"Writers get writer's block," Mr. Fine went on. "And painters get painter's block. Sounds like Jenny's got a case of dollmaker's block."

"Do you catch it like a cold?" Crystal asked.

"Can it kill you?" added Raymond.

"Definitely not fatal," Mr. Fine assured them. "Jenny's run out of ideas for her dolls."

"How can we help?" asked Crystal.

Amy was still worried for Aunt Jenny, but a warm feeling began growing inside her as soon as she heard Crystal use the word *we*.

"Perhaps you should find another artist to ask," suggested Mrs. Fine.

Crystal, Raymond, and Amy sat at the edge of the ocean letting the lazy ends of the waves play hide-and-seek with their legs. They couldn't think of anyone they knew who wrote books or painted. Raymond wanted to send a letter to the person who wrote his favorite story, *The Little Mermaid*, but Crystal said it would take too long to get an answer.

"Besides," Amy added, "Hans Christian Andersen died forever ago."

Giving up, they headed back to the splintery boardwalk. Mattie Stone and Mrs. Goldman waved from their bench.

"I can't believe we don't know one artist," Crystal complained.

We! There was that word again. Amy felt like a starfish that was becoming whole. Maybe Crystal finally wanted to be friends.

"I beg your pardon." Mattie Stone grabbed Crystal's arm as they passed. "Mrs. Goldman and I both think of ourselves as artists."

"You do?" asked Raymond.

"We do?" echoed Mrs. Goldman.

"Why yes," said Mattie Stone. "We're artists with food."

"I suppose we are." Mrs. Goldman nodded. "Why, are you hungry, my *bubbies?*"

"No, we need to ask a question." Amy took a seat between the two women, while Crystal and Raymond made bookends on either side. "Have you ever had a cooking block?"

"You've seen the lovely butcher block where I do my chopping," Mrs. Goldman said.

"She means like having no ideas on what to cook for dinner," Crystal explained. "Or not feeling like baking for days and days."

"Never happens," Mattie Stone snapped. "I walk in the kitchen, and I'm inspired."

Mrs. Goldman was quiet. "Sometimes . . . ," she said slowly. "Nothing I can think of to cook seems right."

48

"What do you do?" asked Crystal.

"Do you send out for Chinese food?" Raymond put in.

Mrs. Goldman smiled and patted Raymond's cheek. "On a bad day, *bubeleh*, maybe. But if I want to try to think of something delicious for when my little friends come to visit, I go to the market and buy wonderful ingredients to get me going again."

"Ingredients," Crystal repeated. She leaned over to Amy and nodded. "That's it."

They started to go off the boardwalk, but Raymond lagged a little.

"Can't we go with Mrs. Goldman for a snack?" he begged.

"Miz Martin probably just needs more socks and things," said Crystal.

"I can't believe I didn't think of it," Amy admitted. "Last time I looked in Aunt Jenny's scrap basket, all the socks were tan. Maybe she hates tan."

"Don't worry." Crystal walked slightly ahead. "I know just what we gotta do."

Sock Heaven

Raymond and Amy waited while Crystal ran inside to get her mama's laundry basket. Then they followed as she walked along the side of Mattie Stone's house.

"What does Mama always say about socks on laundry day?" Crystal quizzed Raymond.

"'One sock from each wash gets stolen away to sock heaven,'" he recited.

Sock heaven. Amy softly repeated the words that sounded like the start of a special prayer for Aunt Jenny. And as they rounded their way into Mattie Stone's yard, it seemed as though sock heaven, that wondrous place, was before her.

Socks and stockings in every imaginable color and pattern hung on a huge web of clotheslines. They reminded Amy of the flags of the world,

swaying proud and beautiful in front of the United Nations back home in New York.

The three raced toward the streams of color. The clothes were warm to their touch and smelled like sunlight and lilacs. Amy longed to pull them down in piles like brilliant fall leaves.

"Listen," Crystal whispered. "If everybody always loses a sock in the wash like Mama says, no one will notice if we take one from each yard."

Raymond shook his head. "Stealing," he said solemnly.

Amy felt her fingers tingle, anxious to choose just the right one. "According to your mama, Mattie Stone's gonna lose a sock anyway."

"That could make two if we take one," Raymond pointed out.

Crystal rolled her eyes at her brother. "All sock heaven means is people expect to lose socks. It just happens."

Amy chose a red velvet anklet from Mattie Stone's line and placed it in the laundry basket. Crystal picked a purple paisley knee-high from Mrs. Goldman's and did the same. At the Fines', Crystal and Amy debated taking one or two socks. In the end, they decided on one from each person.

"She's gonna be so happy," Amy said when they reached Aunt Jenny's walk.

"She'll need a whole new house for all the dolls she's gonna make," Raymond put in.

"Stay here," Crystal called, sprinting toward her front door. When she came back, she had an orange-and-black knee-high of her own and a sweat sock of Raymond's.

"Thanks!" Amy beamed at Crystal.

"We can't find the matches anyway," Crystal said with a shrug.

"Gone to sock heaven," added Raymond.

The One-Sock Wonders

Amy waited until after she and Aunt Jenny finished their tuna sandwich supper to bring out her surprise. "Look, Aunt Jenny. These must have fallen behind the scrap basket."

Aunt Jenny laid each sock on her lap to admire as though it were a strand of fine pearls. "It's going to be a nice night." She glanced up at Amy. "Why don't you grab a book, and I'll take my sewing out to the swing."

"Okay," Amy agreed.

Amy read *Charlotte's Web* to the comforting rhythm of Aunt Jenny's needle and thread. The new doll, Aunt Jenny said, would be a portrait of Amy, with flip-flops made of pipe cleaners and a real Band-Aid dangling from its knee.

"This sock is the exact blue of your bathing suit," Aunt Jenny pointed out, "and I have just the right yarn for your hair."

"So, you're sewing again," Mr. Fine called from the sidewalk. He and Mrs. Fine were standing arm in arm with Mattie Stone and Mrs. Goldman.

Aunt Jenny shook her head. "You're something else, Arthur," she shouted back. "Did you hear my needle poking through cotton?"

"No, but I heard you biting the thread. Bad for the teeth," he teased. "I'm going to save up and buy you a pair of scissors."

Amy thought the old people would unlink their arms and continue their stroll. Instead they began humming the cancan and kicking their legs like the New York Rockettes.

"I have to see what those nuts are up to," Aunt Jenny said.

Amy had a bad feeling, but she followed Aunt Jenny anyway. Crystal and Raymond and their parents came down to the street as well.

"We're calling ourselves the One-Sock Wonders," Mrs. Fine said. "What do you think, kids?"

The dancers continued to kick up their legs. Each was wearing only one sock—mates to the very ones Aunt Jenny had just been sewing. Finally, they stood still.

For a moment that felt like an hour, everyone stared at each other.

"We didn't think you'd notice," Amy mumbled to her flip-flops.

The old people simply listened.

"We were worried about Miz Martin," Crystal added.

The ocean let out four long moans before anyone spoke again.

"We could give them back," Raymond suggested.

"Too late for that," Mrs. Fine pointed out. She held up the Amy doll Aunt Jenny had started. "Look how lovely this is already."

Usually, Crystal and Raymond got summerwarm smiles from their mama, but now there were storm clouds in her eyes. "You mean to tell me you stole from these good people?" she asked them.

They nodded.

"You can each expect a written apology from these two," their dad told the old people. Then he turned to Crystal and Raymond. "Right now we're going to have a long talk. March!"

Amy saw Crystal and Raymond nervously join hands as they led the way home.

"We better go too," Mr. Fine said to the others. "Especially if the One-Sock Wonders want to make their next audition."

With everyone gone, Aunt Jenny sat Amy back on the porch swing. "So, you were trying to help me, is that right?"

Amy nodded to her flip-flops.

"I appreciate that, Amy, I do. But do you really think I'd want you to borrow like that from my friends?"

"Steal," Amy corrected her. "We stole from them."

"Hey." Aunt Jenny tapped her on the head with the new sock doll. "I'm the one doing the scolding here. That means I'm the one who gets to choose the words."

"Sorry," Amy mumbled.

"That's the word I'd choose," Aunt Jenny said. "Now go say it to the people you 'borrowed' from."

Amy found the old people gathered on the Fines' porch. "I'm really sorry," she told them.

Mr. Fine tried hard to look stern. Instead, he coughed up a chuckle.

"It's not funny, Arthur," Mattie Stone said.

But Amy noticed she was smiling too. And Mrs. Fine was hiding a grin behind her fingers.

"You're not angry at me?"

"Of course not, *bubeleh*," Mrs. Goldman answered.

Mattie Stone kicked off her sandal and bent to peel the red velvet anklet off her foot. "Might as well give your great-aunt Jenny this," she sighed. "It's no good to me now."

Nodding, the others took off their socks and passed them to Amy.

Mrs. Goldman took Amy's hands in hers, socks and all. "Just promise me, if you ever need something again, you'll come to us and ask."

Amy promised.

On her way back to Aunt Jenny's, Amy stopped at Crystal and Raymond's.

"They weren't really mad," she explained as she stood in their doorway. "They kind of thought it was funny." Amy showed them the socks, curled in her hands like a crushed bouquet, and looked up surprised when they didn't say anything.

"Fine for you," Crystal said finally. "We can't come out of the house for the rest of the week."

"We're grounded," Raymond put in. For the first time ever, his voice was as chilly as his sister's. "All because we tried to help you."

"But . . . " Amy's throat tightened. "We did it for Aunt Jenny."

"Doesn't matter," Crystal answered. "Mama says stealing's stealing."

"Told you," Raymond mumbled, earning a glare from his sister.

"What about sock heaven?" Amy started to ask. But the door to Crystal and Raymond's was already closed.

ELEVEN

Empty Spaces

Everybody always makes sand castles or tunnels," Amy said. "Let's do something different, like a person."

"Wonderful idea," Mr. Fine exclaimed. Rascal flapped his tail as though he agreed.

Mr. Fine scooped damp sand into round balls, then stacked them into a form like a small snowman. Amy found thin strips of driftwood for arms. Together they gathered small shells to pattern the eyes and mouth, as Amy had seen Mrs. Goldman do with raisins on her gingerbread men.

"Hey," Amy called. "How about beach glass for earrings?"

Mr. Fine fingered the smooth shapes she had pressed where the ears would be. "You're quite an artist," he said. "It runs in the family."

"Aunt Jenny made me a doll that looks just like me," Amy told him. "And now I think she's making Crystal and Raymond."

"Is that right?" Mr. Fine asked.

"Everyone still thinks Crystal and me are best friends." Amy drew a pocket on their sand person's jacket. "We almost were friends too, but she blames me for getting her grounded."

"You know, Crystal did have a best friend here last summer," Mr. Fine told her. "Mattie Stone's granddaughter from Oklahoma. They did everything together."

"So it's just me she hates," Amy grumbled.

"Torrie Stone really hurt her feelings," Mr. Fine continued. "They promised to write each other and take turns calling once a month. But Torrie never called, and she didn't answer Crystal's letters."

"That's sad," Amy said. Secretly she felt glad, in a mean sort of way, only because Crystal was mad at her.

Mr. Fine rested a hand on Amy's shoulder. "I guess you could say Crystal has her empty spaces, just like the rest of us starfish."

Amy thought about that as Rascal led them back across the sand. Mr. Fine had filled the empty space of her morning. Maybe Crystal and Raymond would forgive her if she could find a way to fill the empty space of their long days inside.

Back on the splintery boardwalk, the audience sat waiting.

"Just look at them," said Mrs. Goldman.

"Like two children," added Mattie Stone in her floppy hat. "Afternoon already, and they've done nothing but play."

Play. Amy knew Crystal and Raymond weren't allowed to have company, but maybe if she stayed on their stoop and they sat by the downstairs window they could play anyway.

Raymond forgave her the moment Amy showed up with her Clue game. She slipped three face-down cards in the top secret envelope, dealt the rest without looking, and passed Raymond's half through the open window. Crystal couldn't be convinced that Amy wasn't cheating.

"I'll be up in my room reading," Amy heard her tell Raymond.

Raymond was Professor Plum and Amy was Miss Scarlet. They

both had game boards, so they could roll their own dice and tell each other which rooms they landed in. Raymond played pretty well considering how little he was, except he needed a lot of help with the spelling.

"What letter does Mustard start with again?" he asked.

"M." Amy studied the cross marks on her Clue pad. "But it's not Colonel Mustard. How about Mrs. White with a wrench in the conservatory," she tried.

"If conser-very starts with a C, she didn't do it in there," Raymond answered.

At first, it seemed funny not to see his face as they played, but after a while, it made Amy less shy about talking.

"I wish Crystal wanted to play with us," she admitted.

"Yeah. This is her favorite game."

"Mine too," she told him. Amy couldn't help feeling she and Crystal were meant to be friends. "Do you think she'll ever like me?" The question was already out when Amy realized Crystal could be listening.

"I don't know," Raymond answered. "But I do."

It made Amy smile and feel sad at the same

time. She stared at Crystal's upstairs window. The curtain was closed, but she thought she saw a shadow shifting.

"You there?" Raymond called out.

Amy picked up the tiny silver candlestick from her Clue board and rolled it in her fingers. She still felt so lonely.

"Hello?" Raymond tried again.

"Mrs. White with a wrench in the billiard room," she said.

"Crystal and I are having a really great time," Amy told her mom. "She says she's never had a best friend before."

Dust was beginning to soften the surfaces at Aunt Jenny's house when Amy discovered two new dolls on her night stand. As she'd expected, one was a boy in a backwards cap with a stripe of zinc on his nose like icing. The other was a long-legged girl, her hair beaded and braided in a quilted pattern.

Crystal and Raymond dolls, with gleaming brown button eyes, resting against the Amy doll in flip-flops. The perfect keepsake from her first summer away, if only they all were really friends.

CHAPTER TWELVE

Starfish Arms

That evening, Amy flipped restlessly through *Little Women* while Aunt Jenny sorted through yarn scraps. Finally the phone rang, and Mrs. Goldman invited them over for an after-supper get-together. Amy pictured the small yellow kitchen filled with women all talking at once like a radio between stations, and she felt less lonely. But Aunt Jenny told Mrs. Goldman she wanted to stay home and sew.

"Why don't you go anyway?" she suggested to Amy. "I know I'm not much company tonight."

When Amy let herself into Mrs. Goldman's house, Mrs. Fine was the only other visitor. Instead of the comforting buzz she'd expected, the kitchen was quiet.

"This is wonderful lemonade, my dear," Mrs. Fine told Mrs. Goldman. She poured some for Amy.

"Why thank you." Mrs. Goldman opened a box of shortbread cookies. "You must have some of these, my darling."

They sounded like Crystal serving chocolate sand surprise by the water, Amy thought glumly. "You guys talk like royalty," she said.

"I feel like a queen when my dear friend comes to visit," Mrs. Goldman answered.

"And I feel like a duchess in her good company as well," added Mrs. Fine.

Despite herself, Amy smiled, thinking of Mrs. Goldman as a queen in her faded housedress and Mrs. Fine a duchess in men's overalls. "Have you been friends a long time?" she asked them.

"Forty-three years," Mrs. Fine announced proudly.

Mrs. Goldman shook her head as she cut into a crumbly coffee cake. "It seems like only a week ago you moved in across the street with that handsome young husband."

"I always envied her cooking," Mrs. Fine confided, helping herself to a slice of coffee cake.

"I don't know what I would have done without

her when Mr. Goldman died." Mrs. Goldman squeezed her friend's hand.

"Me? What did I do?" Mrs. Fine asked Amy.

"She was so brave. Mistress of the situation."

"For a while I was afraid to get close to anyone. Afraid they'd disappear just like my Joe did." Mrs. Goldman stared at the wall with shiny distant eyes. Amy knew she was picturing her husband. "But my friend here bullied me into sitting on the sunny boardwalk instead of alone in the dark house. She stopped me from feeling empty."

Amy had been nibbling on shortbread, but she paused mid-chew. "Mrs. Fine's your starfish arm!"

She was beginning to understand what Mr. Fine had been trying to tell her. Maybe Crystal didn't hate her. Maybe she was just afraid in the way Mrs. Goldman used to be. Afraid to fill her empty space, only to have the friend she'd filled it with disappear again.

"She's my what, *bubeleh?*" Mrs. Goldman asked.

"I'm your starfish arm." Mrs. Fine winked at Amy across the table. "Clearly someone's been talking to my Arthur."

* * *

Amy ran home to Aunt Jenny's to grab her beach bag with the starfish in it, then marched next door before her courage faded.

"Go on up," Crystal and Raymond's dad said. "Tonight's the last night of their punishment anyway. I think they're ready for company."

Raymond was sprawled on the floor with a jigsaw puzzle.

"Hey!" He beamed at Amy.

Crystal sat cross-legged on her bed, flipping TV channels with the sound turned down.

"What is *she* doing here?" she asked a lady on a car commercial.

"I wanted you to see this." Amy passed the starfish to Raymond.

"Can I keep it?" Raymond asked.

"You can share it with Crystal," she answered.

Crystal turned the TV off and glared at Amy. "I've seen an old starfish before."

Amy's cheeks grew hot. "There's something magic about it," she managed to say.

"Really?" Raymond's eyes widened.

"She's cracked," Crystal told him.

Crystal was making this so hard. Amy crouched on the floor and spoke only to Raymond. "Mr. Fine told me that if a starfish loses an arm while it's alive it can grow another one."

"Could I grow one if my arm fell off?" he asked.

"Unh-unh. That's what makes starfish sort of magic. But something like it happens to people."

Raymond leaned against Amy as though she were telling him a bedtime story.

"Like if you or Crystal knew someone and then you didn't know them anymore. They'd leave an empty space. But it wouldn't have to stay empty. You could let someone else fill it." Amy took a deep breath and blurted to Crystal, "I'm not Torrie Stone, and just because she didn't stay your friend doesn't mean I'd do the same thing."

Now that it was said, Amy pulled at the Band-Aid on her knee and waited. She heard the

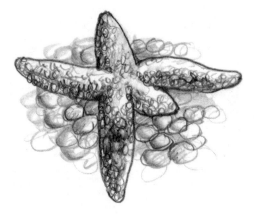

ocean through the open window, as if the sound had been turned off and someone had flicked the switch to On again.

Finally Raymond broke into the silence. "What's that got to do with arms falling off?"

Amy sighed, giving up. "Nothing. I better go."

"She's saying the starfish could grow a new arm now."

Amy stared at Crystal.

"It could?" Raymond turned the starfish in a circle in his hand. "Where? It's got all its arms."

Crystal pointed her chin toward Amy. "She's saying she'll be the new arm if we want her to."

"I don't get it," Raymond mumbled.

Crystal rested her hands on her hips, studying Amy. "Raymond and I are gonna be at the beach tomorrow," she told her. "You can come if you want."

It was the closest Amy had ever gotten to an invitation from Crystal. Still, she wanted to be more than just a tag-along.

"Okay." Amy kept her eyes from drifting toward her flip-flops. "I even thought up a new beach game we could play."

THIRTEEN

Tired of Excuses

Amy sat mashing cornflakes with the back of her spoon and flattening banana slices into putty.

"What a delicious-looking breakfast," Aunt Jenny commented, coming into the kitchen. "For someone with no teeth, that is."

"Morning, Aunt Jenny. I was just busy thinking."

Aunt Jenny poured them each a glass of juice and joined Amy at the table. "I'm a pretty good listener," she offered.

"Crystal asked me to play at the beach with her and Raymond," Amy mumbled to her cereal bowl.

"Isn't that something you do every day?" Aunt Jenny asked.

"Unh-unh. It just looks that way because we're all always there. Mostly Crystal ignores me."

Aunt Jenny's eyebrows lifted into question marks, but all she said was, "I see."

"So I said I'd meet them," Amy continued, "and that I had an idea for a great new beach game." She went back to mashing cornflakes. "I don't really have an idea, though."

"Arthur tells me you make up very imaginative beach games. I'm sure you'll think of something."

"It's easy to plan games for Mr. Fine." Amy sighed. "He says everything I do is wonderful."

"Crystal *is* a tougher audience," Aunt Jenny agreed. "I think you just need to get your creativity flowing." She sipped her juice thoughtfully. "When you kids helped me out of my doll-making funk, what was it you figured out I needed? Ingredients?"

Amy played with a spoonful of cornflake mush and nodded.

"Ingredients . . . " Aunt Jenny cleared the table, adding their dishes to the already full kitchen sink. "Follow me," she said. "I may have just the ingredients you need."

* * *

A trunk made of sweet-smelling wood stood in a corner of Aunt Jenny's bedroom. After clearing a family of dolls off the top, she opened it up. "These are toys from when your mother spent her summers here. Let's see if there's anything inspiring."

They pulled out pails, shovels, Tupperware cups in assorted sizes, a tired old Barbie, and parts of a train set. Amy stared at the pile, but it didn't inspire her. Instead, it made her wish she could go back to bed. She'd pull the covers all the way up and use Aunt Jenny's fall-asleep trick of turning the unfamiliar into the familiar to forget about impressing Crystal.

The unfamiliar into the familiar. Amy grinned at Aunt Jenny and gathered the toys in her beach towel. "I think I've got it," she said.

At the water's edge, Crystal eyed the supply pile coolly. "So what are we doing?" she asked in a bored voice.

Amy announced her plan. "We're gonna build New York City."

"Oh, brother," Crystal mumbled.

Pretending not to hear, Amy started Raymond

on a hole for the subway. He laid the tracks and put the train cars on them. Amy covered it all with sand.

"It's underground," she explained.

Raymond buried a pail of ocean water to be the river, while Amy built a mound beside it. "Liberty Island," she told him, placing Barbie on top.

"That's the Statue of Liberty?" Raymond looked doubtful.

"Maybe if we put her arm up," Crystal suggested, plopping down next to them.

Amy gave Crystal a wide smile, thrilled that she was joining in. "Next we can shape the buildings with these Tupperware cups."

"What are the buildings in New York like?" Crystal asked as they worked.

"Tall and skinny and bunched next to each other," Amy said.

Finally, they stepped back.

"Well?" Crystal turned to Amy. "Does it look like New York?"

Amy studied the sand lumps. They didn't look like anything.

"Well?" echoed Raymond.

"It's gray." Amy sighed. She couldn't even come up with a decent beach game. "New York is gray."

But Crystal just rolled her eyes and laughed. Then they buried their feet in the New York City skyline.

"Let's bury Amy next," Raymond called out. He took handfuls of thick damp sand and patted them over Amy's legs while Crystal scooped out a wall along her side. They covered her up to the neck, smoothing the sand with the palms of their hands as though brushing crumbs from a table.

"We can't hardly see you," Raymond said proudly.

Amy sank down, loving the feel of the beach hugging her shoulders.

"It's my turn to choose a game," she heard Crystal say.

"Tickle bottom?" Raymond asked.

"No." Crystal paused before she announced,

"I think we should teach Amy to ride a bicycle."

Amy sat up, sand breaking and falling, an avalanche all around her. Did Crystal *really* want to teach her to ride, or was she just making fun of her?

"Bike riding's a sidewalk thing," she snapped. "I'm here to do beach stuff."

"After you learn, you can ride on the boardwalk," Raymond said. "That would count as beach stuff."

Amy started to gather her things. "I think Aunt Jenny needs me to do something," she told the sandy Barbie in her hand.

"Can't you do it later?" Crystal asked.

"We'll even help," Raymond added.

The two of them stood there, studying her. The ocean seemed to be whispering about her to the sand.

No matter what Crystal's reasons were, Amy decided, she was tired of her own dumb mama's-girl excuses.

"Okay." She took a deep breath and let it out slowly. "Teach me."

FOURTEEN

Brave

Put on this helmet," Crystal ordered. "You can use my bike if you want, but Raymond's would probably be better."

Nodding, Amy straddled the smaller one.

Crystal sat on the front fender, facing her. "You won't fall."

Amy felt trapped. "Not as long as you stay there," she couldn't help answering.

Raymond gave a push from the back while Crystal used her legs as brakes. The bike crawled forward.

"This is okay," Amy said, getting used to the feel.

"Good." Crystal signaled for Raymond to stop pushing. "I'm going in back with Raymond."

Without Crystal blocking her view, the dead-end beach block seemed to stretch into a major road. Slowly the street moved backward beneath her again.

"You won't let go?" Amy called, afraid to look back.

"Don't worry," Crystal answered.

Amy heard the slapping of their sneakers as the street wobbled and picked up speed.

"Still here," an out-of-breath Raymond assured her.

Amy relaxed a little and felt the first breeze of the day, salty and cool, as a whirring rhythm hummed from the pedals. She passed the gray blur of Mrs. Goldman's house and the blue blur of the Fines'. That's when she realized Crystal and Raymond were half a block away.

"I'm doing it," Amy said, and the bike grew shaky beneath her. "I'm doing it," she repeated, and she steadied out again.

She passed Aunt Jenny's house, where she imagined an audience of sock dolls cheering from the windows.

Amy circled the street over and over. "I can't believe it," she called when she passed Crystal and Raymond. The bike was almost light now beneath the sure pump of her feet. "I'm riding a bike!"

Finally her legs grew tired.

Crystal and Raymond hadn't taught her how to stop!

"I want to get off," she cried as she neared them. But they were specks in the distance before she could hear their response.

"Slow down and brake," they shouted as Amy came around again. But in her panic, the words didn't have any meaning. The only thing she could think to do was find something to grab.

Amy veered off the street onto the nearest lawn and reached out for the porch railing. The bike hit the wall and bounced to a stop, throwing Amy onto a bed of pink and lavender.

"You okay?" Crystal and Raymond ran over and pulled the bike off Amy.

"Mattie Stone's prize

garden," she moaned.

"Uh-oh." Raymond covered his mouth.

Crystal plucked at a few crushed flowers. "Mattie Stone will never notice," she said.

Amy studied a bruise blooming on her knee.

"You're all right," Crystal said.

"Just a little black and blue," Amy agreed.

Crystal slung her arm over Amy's shoulder. "It was brave of you to get on the bike like that," she continued.

"I needed training wheels for a year," Raymond put in.

Brave! Amy repeated the word to herself. An hour ago, Amy had still felt like a mama's girl. But Crystal had just called her *brave*.

"Maybe tomorrow we'll give you braking lessons," Crystal told her.

"I can handle that," Amy said in her new brave-person voice.

"You're all right," Crystal said again.

This time, Amy understood. Crystal meant it as a compliment.

FIFTEEN

The Best Day

Crystal, Raymond, and Amy spent the rest of the afternoon playing Clue up in Crystal's room. At suppertime, Aunt Jenny called to Amy through the window.

Amy poked her head out and listened for a minute. "She wants us to go over to her house," she told Crystal and Raymond.

"Did she say why?" Crystal asked as they started next door.

Amy shook her head. "I hope this doesn't mean she tried to cook again."

"Hey!" Raymond pointed to Aunt Jenny's porch, where the old people sat watching the street the way they usually watched the ocean. "It's like they went and moved the boardwalk."

"There you are, kids," Aunt Jenny said. "We're having a party!"

"Whose birthday is it?" Raymond asked, climbing the steps.

"No one's that I know of," Mrs. Fine answered. She ushered them onto the rickety swing while Mrs. Goldman piled plates heavy with food for them.

"I made the latkes and blintzes, and Mrs. Fine brought this delicious cold chicken."

"A-hem." Mattie Stone folded her arms and waited.

"And Mattie has a special gourmet surprise warming in your aunt Jenny's kitchen."

Crystal turned to Aunt Jenny. "Miz Martin, if it's no one's birthday, what are we celebrating?"

Aunt Jenny held up the Amy sock doll. Over its bathing suit was an orange-and-black reflector vest and on its head, a helmet made from a soup ladle. "We're celebrating Amy's new skill of bicycle riding."

Grinning, Crystal and Amy straddled the doll on the arm of the swing as though it were riding a bicycle.

"You're gonna have to throw Amy another party tomorrow," Raymond told the old people. "We're giving her stopping lessons."

"Good," Mattie Stone responded. "I could

live without another bald spot in my garden."

Amy held her breath, expecting a scolding. But Mattie Stone walked past her into the house, stepping over Rascal, who was snoozing, off duty, in the doorway.

Aunt Jenny placed Mr. Fine's cassette recorder on the food table and pressed the Play button. Old-fashioned music floated into the air instead of a talking story.

"May I?" Mr. Fine bowed to his wife.

"I thought you'd never ask," Mrs. Fine said, and they began waltzing.

"We ought to do this kind of thing more often," Aunt Jenny said.

"I can't remember the last time I had this much fun," added Mrs. Goldman.

The screen door slammed open, and Mattie Stone put a heavy bowl on the food table. "Children, you have to try this." Amy peeked under the lid and saw her favorite tear-shaped shells, with the watercolor paintings, swimming in a sea of spaghetti sauce.

With a small sharp fork, Mattie Stone plucked a tiny bite of fish and passed it to Amy. It tasted like the beach would, if the beach were sticky and chewy.

"Can I just have the shells after?" she asked when she finally swallowed.

"I guess she got you back for her flowers," Crystal whispered, making Amy giggle.

Mattie Stone stood fussing with the mussel shells. "You know, I almost tripped over that cord on my way to the kitchen," she complained to Aunt Jenny. "What's your phone doing on the windowsill anyway?"

"I moved it so Amy wouldn't miss her call," Aunt Jenny said.

"Well, that was good thinking," Mattie Stone decided. "Especially given the way her mother tends to worry."

Embarrassed, Amy glanced at Crystal. "She only worries because I'm so far away," she explained.

Crystal shrugged. "Our mama worries if we're just on the beach."

"Really?" Amy stared at her.

"She even worries when we're right on the stoop," Raymond added.

Amy shook her head. "My mom's like that too," she admitted.

"Sometimes Mama drives me crazy," Crystal said. "But I still don't know if I could be away from her a whole summer. You ever get homesick, Amy?"

Amy kicked her flip-flops off and on. "A lot."

"Does that mean you hate it here?" Raymond looked worried.

"Unh-unh. I'm homesick, but I'm happy here too," Amy answered, realizing it was true.

Amy finally felt like she and Crystal were friends, but that was just one of the reasons. There was Aunt Jenny and her dolls, Mrs. Goldman's kitchen, Mrs. Fine's winks, even Mattie Stone's hat, and the funny things Raymond always said. And of course, Mr. Fine's eyes—soft, sky-colored marbles that saw her better than anyone.

Nothing could change the fact that, without her mom, Amy felt like a starfish who had lost an arm. It just wasn't so bad anymore, because until it grew back again, she was surrounded by all these other wonderful arms.

The old people were noisily praising the food, but Amy knew they were good at talking and listening at the

same time. "It was really nice of everyone to throw me this party. You're all always really nice to me."

Mr. Fine felt his way over and put his hand on Amy's shoulder. "Well, having you here is nothing less than a gift for us," he told her.

"A dream, *bubeleh*," Mrs. Goldman said.

"An ice-cream cone," added Raymond, which started everyone laughing.

"Hey, Ice-Cream Cone!" called Crystal. "The phone's ringing."

Amy leaned on the sill of the open window so she could stay at the party while she talked on the phone.

"Mom, I've had the best day." The words weren't very different from the ones she used every night, yet saying them felt very different, since she meant them this time. "But if I tell you what I learned to do, you have to promise not to worry. . . ."

Amy's bike-riding sock doll sat on the swing next to Crystal and Raymond, marking that place as hers. Down the block the waves crashed, sounding just like applause.